THE

EXCITEMENT

I

BRING

WARREN C. HOLLOWAY
"AMERICA'S NEW STORYTELLER"

GOOD 2 GO PUBLISHING

THE EXCITEMENT I BRING
Written by WARREN C. HOLLOWAY
Cover Design: Davida Baldwin, Odd Ball Designs
Typesetter: Mychea
ISBN: 978-1-947340-53-4
Copyright © 2020 Good2Go Publishing
Published 2020 by Good2Go Publishing
7311 W. Glass Lane • Laveen, AZ 85339
www.good2gopublishing.com
https://twitter.com/good2gobooks
G2G@good2gopublishing.com
www.facebook.com/good2gopublishing
www.instagram.com/good2gopublishing

PROLOGUE

"Imagine wanting and yearning for something or someone so much yet having the power to resist it or them right when that moment of euphoria is about to appease your desires. Now place that one person you have in mind in your presence right now, along with one hundred million dollars. Would all that you've been yearning for and desire shift to deception, wanting the obvious, or would the obvious be something or someone you've always desired?"

ONE

"Welcome to Custom Body Fitness, ladies,"

Jaelen Jones said, greeting all of the women

entering his gym that catered to women only,

giving them their privacy without having men

always approaching them while they were trying

to work out. "I'm Jaelen Jones, the owner and

operator of this gym. I will be the only male here;

however, my focus is on getting you ladies the bodies you all want and are willing to work for.

We also offer energy drinks, shakes, and bars over at the counter with Deborah, my assistant."

Deborah, the five-foot-ten woman with an in-shape CrossFit body, light blond hair, glowing blue eyes, and a smile, welcomed the ladies as she waved at them. Jaelen continued addressing the women. "Today we're going to focus on the glutes and thighs, followed by the stomach. I know you ladies want to keep it tight for your men, even you single ladies wanting to attract, or you all are here simply to get fit. Which is even better since no one will appreciate you until you start appreciating you," he said, getting the women to nod their heads in acknowledgement of his words.

Jaelen Jones was a twenty-four-year-old Afro-American with a close hair cut faded on the side, clean-shaven displaying his baby face looks that flowed with his light green eyes that seemed to distract some of the women, especially the first timers here at the gym. Jaelen, standing six foot two, towered over all of the women present. His fit frame could easily be seen with the tight blue tank top that read, "Custom Body Fitness—the best way to your new body."

Jaelen, being college smart, had majored in psychology, which allowed him to have social skills and read people. However, it wasn't for him, so he opted to do what he loved: exercise and be around people who embraced his gift as an instructor who knows exactly what it takes to get the body they need. His reviews online were four and five stars out of five. This, accompanied by word of mouth and social media retweets, allowed him to stay booked. Most of the women came just to see him, wishing they could get his attention. He knew this, but never wanted to allow this to hinder him or his business.

"Ladies, we're going to do a ten-down exercise, starting with ten squats followed by ten jumping jacks. This is what I call 'build and burn.' We're going to build the muscle while burning the fat. By the time this ninety-day cycle is finished, each of you young ladies will have a body that makes you feel good about you. It will also make you enjoy taking selfies if you're not taking enough of them already," he said, getting the women to laugh. He started displaying the exercise to them, counting down. This was the first of a few exercises he had in mind for the ladies today.

Thirty minutes into the workout, he made his way around the gym to speak with every client, making them feel comfortable with his words of encouragement.

"You're doing good, Mrs. Liuen."

"Please call me Danna. The 'Mrs.' thing is for my kids' friends and public places, not the gym. Besides, Danna makes me feel younger," the forty-seven-year-old Asian beauty said, standing five foot one and weighing a medium-built 135 pounds. She was heavy compared to the 105 pounds she weighed when she got married twenty years ago. Now with three kids

ranging from fourteen to nineteen, she wanted

her body back. She wanted her husband to look

at her as he once did, when they met, or as he

did before she had the three kids.

"Okay, Danna, when you run in place, I want

your legs to come a little higher, because this

tightens the stomach muscles right here," he

said, placing his hand on the side, then on her

abdomen. "When you raise your legs, you start

to feel it in your glutes; it also tightens it up right

here. This is the target we're all focusing on

today," he said, placing his hand professionally,

no different than a doctor assessing his patient.

Jaelen strategically assessed Danna before walking away to the next client. Danna didn't want him to walk away. His touch, although professional, gave her comfort. Maybe it was because her husband was always on the go, funding the chain of growing supermarkets. When he came in from working all day, he only had time for a shower, a quick meal, and sleep.

"Am I doing this right, Mr. Jones?" Paula Snyder asked. Paula, a small-town woman, was raised in Mechanicsburg, Pennsylvania. She now resided in Harrisburg close to her fiancé's car lots. Paula just turned forty-four, but she looked well-kept with her glowing tan, hazel-brown eyes, and dark brown silky hair that easily flowed over her shoulders when she's not working out. Right now, she had it pulled back, exposing her naturally beautiful face with a mole above the left side of her top lip, adding to her sex appeal. Not that she needed much with her perky 36C breast implants, preserving her youth by any means.

"Yes, that is right. Now, ladies, switch to the lunges I was showing you earlier," he said, still standing at Paula's side. "Step into the lunge so you can feel the stretch and burn at the same time. We're looking for that burn because it's how we build the muscles and shake the unwanted fat," he said, placing his hand on the small of her back. "Can you feel it right here?" he asked, lowering his hand to her bottom. "It should be tightening with each deep step into the lunge," he added. She closed her eyes, thinking of his choice of words each deep step. She was thinking of something else, especially since her fiancé of three years seemed to be stringing her along. This was why she was here: to get fit either to make him see that they should be married or to make him regret not following through on his commitment of proposing to her three years ago. A part of her believed he had proposed to silence her about commitment, since they were together four years before he put the ring on her finger. Now three years after the proposal she still wanted what she was promised. "You make this look easy, Paula," Jaelen said, continuing to make his way past a few ladies, nodding his head smiling at each one, allowing them to know they were doing well. They were all sweating, looking tired and ready to quit, but they still pushed through knowing the end result would be the custom body they had come for.

Jaelen noticed another female amongst the twenty-four women in the class. This female already looked fit. She also seemed to know what she was doing already, as if she had watched his online exercise videos. He walked past her to see if he recognized her from a previous class, but nothing. She didn't even look up at him, being so focused on her workout. He could tell from the intensity in her look, but she still looked good as the beads of sweat flowed off her forehead. Her jet-black hair was pulled back, illuminating gray eyes. She had perfectly tweezed lined black eyebrows that made her eyes pop even more. Her full lips were heart shaped and kissable for the love interest in her life, which was her husband, from the looks of the four-carat solitary diamond on her finger with the encrusted diamond wedding band. It didn't look cheap; neither did her Prada yoga pants with the pink top.

"You're doing a very good job, ma'am," Jaelen said, not knowing her name, though she'd been there a few times already. This got her attention, being addressed as ma'am, when she was younger than the first two women he had spoken to. She glanced up at him briefly before focusing back on her exercises. He continued on, making his way back to the front

of the class. The timer on his Fitbit went off

allowing him to know that the class's time was

up. "That's time, ladies. Take a deep breath.

Now let it out. Another deep breath, relax, and

let it out. You young ladies should feel proud of

yourselves for being another step closer to that

custom body you deserve. I thank you all for

coming out. Tell a friend to tell a friend about my

class and the results you get following my diet

and workout plan. Deborah will have all of your

custom protein or energy drinks over there. This

will refuel your bodies, allowing your muscles to

recoup faster," he said, watching the ladies grab

their things and then their preferred drinks. He stood by the door wishing them well and encouraging them. "I look forward to seeing you all tomorrow or as scheduled. You deserve a better version of you."

The Italian female he'd had his eye on at the end of the class was coming up next to leave, drinking her shake in between wiping the sweat from her face. Her natural beauty backed by the look of intrigue in her eyes made him want to know more about her. She was not like anyone he had ever come across. "Why is she here?" he wondered, with her looking as fit as she did.

She continued walking as if she didn't see him.

He couldn't let this happen.

"Have a nice day, ma'am. I look forward to seeing you again," he said with a smile, knowing it would make her halt, and it did, with her taking offense to the "ma'am" thing.

"Ma'am isn't always the best approach," she said, eying him.

"I'm sorry, I didn't mean to offend you Mrs.?"

"Patrones. Laila Patrones, either one is fine. I like your place here. It's different. I can actually work out without being hounded by men who come to gyms just for that, as if they don't see this from across the room," she said, holding up

her four-carat diamond solitary backed by her

diamond-encrusted wedding band. A stop sign

to most men, but a welcoming sign to those who

are intrigued by such caliber women.

"Well, Mrs. Patrones, I thank you for coming

in today. I do look forward to seeing you come

again."

"You have my business. I'll even recommend

you to a few women I know can spend some

time here," she said nodding, giving a brief smile

before exiting. She intrigued him because she

was unlike many other customers that came to

his gym. She caught his full attention, yet she seemed to be hard to get, especially with making it known that she didn't wish to be hit on.

"What's she uptight about?" Paula asked, sipping her energy drink. She was trying to make small talk, something Jaelen picked up on quickly, especially with the look in her eyes peeking above her cup as she drank.

"She was telling me how she likes the place, that's all," he said, not wanting to get into other customers' business with other clients. As he spoke, he also was eyeing Paula's engagement ring, two carats in the middle of one-carat flawless diamonds. She caught his eye glancing at the ring, so she addressed it.

"Some promises are never fulfilled," she said. His eyebrows turned up wondering what she meant. At the same time he found her upfront bluntness quite interesting.

"I don't understand, please explain, so I don't make the same mistake in my life," he said.

"I've been engaged for three years with no preparations to get married. I even started hinting to him that I'm working out to get ready to fit in my wedding dress with the hope this would get him on board with my vision, but he's too consumed with his work."

"Patience can sometimes be the greatest reward, allowing you to get what you really want and deserve in the end." His words sent a stimulating calm over her as she dissected his words that seemed to be spoken just for her. Her eyes were smiling back at him, not realizing that her face was also smiling as she slipped into a thought of him being the reward for her patience in the end.

"Well, Ms. Snyder, I look forward to seeing you again so you can achieve the physical goals you're looking for."

"I do have a new inspiration to get this body fit even if it's not for a wedding dress. I'm going to be the best me I can be," she said, waving bye before walking away, leaving him to capture her curvaceous bottom with extra bounce since she knew he would be looking.

"Eeh hmm. You done over there?" Deborah, his assistant, asked, seeing that the women all seemed to be losing sight of why they came here once they saw Jaelen.

"Yeah, I'm done. You know it's my ritual to greet and send the customers off each day. This is what separates us from the other trainers and gyms. I build a personal professional connection with them to make them feel comfortable about working out in their own skin, and not be bashful."

"No one is around, so you can save the professional commercial pitch for someone you're selling the idea of this gym to. I know what these women think and how you can be a player if you like."

"I keep it clean here, and you know this."

She gave him the side-eye as she wiped the countertop off, before coming around with her bag ready to leave.

"A few of your clients that came in today made appointments for house calls. The one lady that was close to two hundred pounds said she would feel more comfortable in her own home working out instead of being around all of these women that look like they don't need to work out."

"Send me the info. If it interferes with any of my classes, I'll need you to run the class for me," he said, making his way out of the gym. She followed as he locked up everything.

TWO

"See you tomorrow," **Deborah** said, heading toward her car.

Jaelen made his way over to his car, immediately noticing Mrs. Liuen on her phone trying to reach out to her husband to no avail, since she had locked her keys in her car.

"Pick up the phone, Daniel," she yelled into the phone only to get the answering machine. "Honey, I left my keys in the car. Can you please come get me? I'm at the gym," she added before hanging up. She leaned against the red BMW M5 with a plush black leather interior.

"Danna, can I help you with anything?" Jaelen asked, seeing that his client was clearly in distress with having locked her keys in the car. The look on her face was sad, helpless yet innocent. He couldn't get into his G55 Mercedes Benz truck and leave her there to fend for herself or wait until her husband got there.

"I'm okay. I'll wait until he calls me back or gets my message to pick me up," she responded. Jaelen, being a gentleman, felt he couldn't just leave.

"I'll stay until he gets here, because I would feel bad just leaving knowing you're waiting here locked out of your car," he responded. She gave a brief smile before folding her arms and waiting. Then a thought came to her.

"I have an extra set of keys at the house if you don't mind running me by there real quick?" she said, not wanting to wait on her husband.

"Where do you live?"

"Fishing Creek Road," she responded, which was roughly ten minutes from his downtown gym. He checked his watch for time, always wanting to be punctual and sticking to his daily schedule.

"No problem, get in."

She smiled before getting into the truck.

"You're so nice for this. I'll definitely recommend everyone I know to your gym. I don't have many followers, but I know people," she said as he drove off.

They drove close to five minutes before coming to a stoplight. Danna was looking out of the window at the car on their right, only to see

her husband. At first glance, she was excited,

until she saw her husband's hand slide over to

the passenger seat and then a young woman

lean over to him, kissing him on the lips. Her

husband couldn't see her behind the dark tinted

windows of the G55 Benz truck. She sucked in

a mouthful of air, emotional and stressed by the

sight of this, because it was now clear to her why

he wasn't answering his phone. A tear slid down

her face, something Jaelen noticed.

"Is everything okay, Danna?" Just as he

asked, the light turned green, allowing him to

see the Lexus LS450 pull off with an Asian man inside it accompanied by another woman. It didn't take long for him to process what was taking place. The pain in Danna's eyes displayed it all. "You still want me to go to the house?"

"Yes, he won't be going there," she said, texting her husband these words: "I once loved you enough not to hate you; now I hate you enough to stop loving you."

"Don't send that message," Jaelen said. "I know you're hurt right now, but you've been married for some time, correct?"

"Yes."

"Take control of the emotions you're feeling right now. Be in charge of what's happening; therefore, it cannot rob you of your joy, your inner happiness. I don't know what the message says, but I know it's probably not good, which means you're giving him the power over your emotions."

Danna was looking down at her phone as the tears still streamed, falling onto the screen on the phone. She cleared the message and placed her phone back into her bag. Then she put her head back, eyes closed, allowing the pain to stream through her body. At the same time thoughts of getting even to make her husband feel her pain also entered her mind. Jaelen remained quiet until they pulled up to her home, a five thousand-square-foot ranch home with a three-car garage.

"We're here, Danna," he said. She opened her eyes looking on at the house she once viewed as home. She exited the truck making her way into the house to get the keys. Jaelen sat in the truck checking his cell phone for his new clients and looking on his social media accounts to see what his customers were saying and how they were rating him. He also checked his Instagram seeing current and previous customers showing off their new look and giving him praise for his workouts and compatible diets.

Fifteen minutes passed before he looked up from his phone. He looked toward the front door where Danna had entered. Thoughts of her bringing harm to herself entered his mind. This made him exit the truck and race over to the house. As soon as he made it to the front door, he saw the screen door closed but the front door open, allowing him to see in. Danna was on the couch with a bottle of Southern Comfort in front of her taking shots. He entered and went over to her as she downed the third shot, which was taking effect on her little 135-pound frame.

"Danna, this is not taking control of your emotions and the situation," Jaelen said, sliding the bottle back. She raised her head up and wiped the tears in her eyes.

"I needed a little Southern Comfort to help take control," she responded.

Jaelen turned and looked back at the front door wondering if he should leave. No one else was home right now. What else would she do if he left her like this, he questioned.

"Did you find your keys?"

"Yes, but I can't drive now," she responded. He knew this seeing that the one hundred-proof liquor was taking its effect on her. She pulled the bottle back to her pouring another double shot, this time looking at Jaelen with sad eyes.

"I'm feeling in control now," she responded after downing the shot.

"You're actually relinquishing your power, giving up on the most beautiful person in the world, and that's you," he said, trying to encourage her. He knew if he left now, she would attempt to drink the entire bottle until

someone saved her from herself. "Let's go. I'll

help you take control," he said, picking her up.

She found his masculine embrace comforting.

His touch was more than she'd had in some

time. However, Jaelen was simply being a

gleeman, a professional caring for his clients far

outside of the workplace. He took her out to the

truck and placed her in the back seat. "A part of

taking control is you knowing you are worth

more and deserve more in life and in love. You

love your husband because you've stuck around

for as long as you have with him. Now you have

to get past this very instance and rebuild you, in

order to rebuild your marriage, if this is what you truly want," Jaelen said before getting into the front and driving to his place.

Ten minutes later they arrived at his 2,500-square-foot condo lined with all of the amenities of a successful bachelor. He carried Danna into his condo and placed her on the black plush leather love seat.

"Outside of alcohol, can I get you anything to drink or something to eat?"

"I would like to have you poured into a cup so I can drink you up," she said, making him laugh at how this once shy, quiet lady that came to his gym had become so blunt. He was not one to take advantage of the drunk or emotionally damaged. At this point he was remaining professional and caring.

"I'm not one of the choices," he responded, "but I can get you some coffee."

"I get it, I'm an old lady in your eyes, and this body has been around forty-seven years longer than you like."

"No, no, that's not the case here. I'm just trying to be respectful and accommodating you in your time of emotional need," he responded, looking into her sad eyes. "Now with that established, I'm going to take a shower to freshen up before I make something to eat," he said, disappearing into his bedroom and leaving her to her thoughts.

Danna took hold of the remote and turned the TV on, flipping through the channels as her thoughts consumed her. She flashed back to seeing her husband with the other woman, then thought about all she'd given him over the years: love, loyalty, children, and valuable time.

Her eyes veered into the direction Jaelen had vanished. A part of her wondered what it would be like to share his time and space, to have him embrace and hold her with the intention of love and comfort, not in a professional manner as he always carried himself.

The alcohol streaming through her body in full effect made her feel a strong buzz from the multiple shots of one hundred-proof Southern Comfort. The feelings she was having were all over the place, but the one thing she wanted was to feel. She needed to feel something to make her come alive, something to make her escape the pain, to make her feel good inside and out. Most of all, she needed someone to appreciate her true worth. The strange thing was, her alcoholic buzz was making her have thoughts of Jaelen, as wrong and sinful as these thoughts were. She managed to get the courage to stand to her feet. She took a deep breath and slightly staggered in the direction she had seen him go. Her mind and heart started to race with each step.

She entered his bedroom and made her way over to the bathroom, where she heard running water. She stood in the doorway of the bathroom looking on at him behind the glass shower door. Her heart pounded now. She feared rejection, at the same time knowing her next step was welcoming another man into her space that had only been for her husband for the last twenty plus years. All of these thoughts were calmed as images of Jaelen pulling her close to make love to her body entered her mind.

Her clothes came off, falling to the floor and leaving her bare. She took another step, and reaching out to the handle of the shower door, she closed her eyes then slid the door open, before opening her eyes. He looked on at her not saying a word yet taking in all of her beauty.

Her body looked twenty years younger than her forty-seven years of age. She didn't even have any stretch makes from the kids she'd had.

"I need to freshen up too if you don't mind," she said, stepping into the shower and reaching past him for the shampoo. He didn't say a word. His silence added intrigue to this situation that he seemed to be allowing her to take control of.

She started shampooing her hair under the other rain showerhead. The shower also boasted jet sprayers for massaging the body after a long day's work or workout.

As she was rinsing the shampoo from her

hair, she started fantasizing about her hands roaming over Jaelen's body, and his hands over hers finding her tight love spot. Her visions of this seemed so real, placing her into the moment. She could feel him pick her up, thrusting all of himself into her body. The thoughts she was having made it feel so real she didn't even realize she let out a moan. However, it caught Jaelen's attention as he was rinsing off. Her light moan triggered something inside of him, making him turn off the professional courtesy, only to turn on the young pretty boy bachelor.

He took hold of a soft sponge and then the

Dove body wash. Danna still had her back to him with her head under the shower rinsing it when she felt the sponge make contact with her body. She didn't resist. This only enhanced what she was feeling and thinking, making her fantasy of him come alive. He took his time sensually washing her neck, then her shoulders, down her back, over her butt parting down the middle, over her legs, down to her calves, to her feet, carefully tending to each foot, washing them clean. He turned her around only to make his way back up washing the front, parting her legs and coming face-to-face with her close-shaven pretty kitty with the perfect line wax job that exposed her protruding pearl that was pulsating awaiting his intimate touch. However, he continued on washing her body over her belly, up to her still perky breasts, up to her neck. Her eyes were still closed, head back embracing his touch—a touch that she hadn't had from her husband in over seven months. Her heart was pounding turned on by this, feeling the rush of the moment.

"Open your eyes," he said, looking into her eyes and caressing her wet hair. "Are you ready to be truly appreciated?"

A wave of erotic excitement came over her

processing the question, knowing she'd never been intimate with her husband like this, let alone in the shower. Their sex life was in the bed, only at night, in the missionary position.

"Yes, please," she responded, letting out a sensual sigh.

He placed a kiss on her forehead before taking control, turning her around and allowing the shower to rinse off the soap. He caressed her hair to the side, exposing her neck, which he leaned into, placing a love bite. This was another thing she'd never had done. It was turning her on. His masculine fingers glided down her back over her bottom before his large

hands squeezed her butt. He also lowered

himself coming face-to-face with her bottom,

parting her legs and displaying her pretty wax

job. He thrust his tongue into her body, sending

a pulsating sensation of pleasure racing through

her as his fingers assisted caressing her pearl.

"Oooooooh my, ooooooh."

Her husband, for his own reasons, didn't feel

he needed to give her oral. So this was the first

time she'd ever had it done to her, blowing her

mind, taking her by an orgasmic storm the faster

his tongue and fingers moved in and around her

body.

"Oooooh, ooooooh, ooooooh, what's happ-ening, mmmmmmh, mmmmmmh."

He started thrusting his thick, long fingers into her body sending another surging pulsating wave rushing through her body, making her legs shake and at the same time making her stomach clench as this feeling of butterflies was stirring inside of her. Her moans and breathing picked up at the same time she reached out to take hold of the shower safety bar to embrace this orgasmic storm that was racing through her body. However, she hit the button to the jet massaging stream, which came out fast from each direction. Strange as it was, this too turned her on as it hit her now sensitive body from every direction.

Jaelen turned her around coming face-to-face with the pretty pearl, placing his tongue on it while he raised her left leg over his right shoulder. Now he took full control over her body, lashing his tongue over the pearl while his fingers magically assisted this orgasmic foreplay.

"Ooooh my, ooooh my, mmmmmmh, ooooh my, ooooooh, ooooooh," she moaned with her eyes closed, breathing heavily, loving his touch backed by this orgasmic rushing sensation that was making her heart, mind and body race. She could feel herself closing in fast on an eruption. She couldn't hold it back. This powerful feeling was surging through her body making her legs feel weak, shaking as her moan intensified. "Ooooooh, oooooh no, oooooh my, oooooh, ooooooh, ooooooh." Here it came. She couldn't hold back, she'd reached her peak. It couldn't be contained. She was loving how his tongue made her feel. This ultimate orgasm was now erupting from her body over and over, her breathing intense and heavy. Her hands were holding on to the shower racks tightly, embracing this powerful feeling of pleasure. "Ooooooh, ooooooh, ooooh my, ooooooh my."

Jaelen felt her body under his oral spell shaking from the intense streaming of orgasm pulsating through her body. He continued on until he came to a slow caressing motion of her pearl. He slid her leg from his shoulder and looked on at her with her eyes still closed. She was still holding onto the racks. He placed a kiss on her lips, which were just as soft as her love spot. The jet sprayers beat on their bodies massaging them.

"Do you feel appreciated now?" he asked after he pulled back from the kiss.

Her eyes opened. "Yes, mmmh, you did very good to my body. I've never had that done before," she said.

Jaelen shook his head smiling knowing there were many men who neglected this foreplay, which should be a sin in itself.

Danna's hand reached down to feel his long, thick erect stiffness. His thickness and length was way more than her husband's, and she wanted it. She wanted all he had to offer, because thus far he had made her feel good inside and out, allowing her to come alive through the pain she was feeling. In fact, that pain had been suppressed by this orgasmic magic he imposed on her. She didn't even feel one ounce of guilt for what just had taken place, when normally she would have felt guilty if she even looked at another man and found him attractive. But not now: this felt all too good.

"Let's save some for later, to keep it intriguing each time we meet," he said, taking her hand off of him. A part of her was thinking, "No, I want it all now." The other part of her found his response even more gravitating, making her look forward to the next time. He leaned in placing another kiss to her lips, before adding, "This right here will be our best-kept secret. No one needs to know, because I want to keep you safe in your marriage, just as I want to be secure in my position of seeing you as we desire."

"I've never been so glad to lock my keys in the car," she said, still feeling her buzz from the alcohol as well as the orgasmic buzz. He laughed at her comment.

"Let's get out of here before we turn to prunes," he said.

They exited the shower and made their way

into the bedroom, where he gave her boxer shorts and a T-shirt that engulfed her small body, but she made it look good.

"Wait right here, I'll get us something to drink," he said, vanishing into the kitchen only to return a few minutes later with two glasses with orange juice and vodka. "Screwdriver. It's like getting healthy and drunk at the same time," he said, making her smile as she took the glass.

"Thank you, Jaelen, for the drink and for being nice to me and my body," she said, drinking the screwdriver.

"You can watch TV. I'll make you something

to eat," he said, heading back into the kitchen.

She sat drinking her beverage before lying back on his plush bed, reflecting on the shower, a scene she'd replay for the rest of her life since it had never happened to her before. Making her realize how boring her husband was. She smiled thinking about Jaelen's hands flowing over her body before his tongue took her under control. Her eyes closed as she fantasized about more with him. She didn't realize with the level of excitement, drinking, and oral sex, she was emotionally, physically, and mentally drained, forcing her into a deep sleep.

THREE

"Danna! Danna, Wake Up!" She could hear

her name being called but was stuck in this

deep, much-needed sleep that was brought on

by drinking and Jaelen's magic fingers and

tongue. When her eyes opened after being

called for the third time, she could see her

husband standing over the top of her. Right then a jolt of fear of him finding her at Jaelen's place in his bed streamed through her sobering her up from what alcohol remained in her system. Her eyes widened looking back at him at the same time she started processing her environment. She was back at home. But how was this possible, she questioned. She didn't remember leaving Jaelen's place. Was it all a dream? Another question entered her mind as she looked down at the table and saw there was no longer a bottle of Southern Comfort on the table.

"You must have had a good workout at the gym for you to come right in and fall asleep with your workout clothing on," her husband added. Hearing his words made her look down at her clothing; she was no longer in Jaelen's boxer shorts or T-shirt.

"Yes, yes, it was a good workout. How was your day? Did you eat?" she asked, going along with the role of the good wife, at the same time trying to process how she got home or if she was fantasizing about the entire thing.

"No, my love, I'm just fine. I ate already with my coworkers before coming home," he responded. This alone made her realize that part of what she remembered wasn't a dream.

"Coworker my ass. You're full of shit, Daniel," she thought, yet managed to force a vacuous smile before standing to her feet. "I guess I'll get freshened up and then make myself something to eat."

"I'll be in the study if you need me, love," he said, coming around the table placing a kiss on her cheek. She didn't feel the love; in fact, she resented it and became repulsed by his touch.

She couldn't get away from him fast enough, racing toward the bedroom and closing the door behind her. She brought her hair around to her nose and took a whiff. It was his shampoo. She smelled her clothing that should have been sweaty from working out, but it too had been cleaned. She could tell from the Downy fabric softener. She used Gain. She started smiling, relieved that she wasn't losing her mind simply fantasizing about Jaelen. What had taken place wasn't in her mind. It really happened.

She headed to the bathroom and took her clothes off, turning the shower on. Something about the sound of the water crashing down and the steam filtering through the bathroom triggered her thoughts, flashing back to her intimate session with Jaelen. Her eyes looking on at the empty shower envisioned how it all had taken place. She closed her eyes, placing her hand on her neck remembering exactly where he had placed the love bite. She started smiling as she opened her eyes only to realize her fingers were pressing up against her pearl stimulating herself. She halted her act of pleasure, laughing, thinking about how he had made her come alive, feeling young again.

"Danna, you're a good girl gone bad," she said looking into the mirror smiling at herself, at the same time checking out her body that was truly appreciated by someone other than her husband. She entered the shower, cleaning up and at the same time trying to figure out how she got home. This part of her time with Jaelen made him even more of a mystery, yet a distinguished gentleman for his acts of kindness thinking about her and her marriage.

Danna didn't realize that when she had passed out in his bed, he took the time to wash her things and then dressed her before bringing her home. He knew he couldn't wait until she woke up because that would be in the morning with the number of shots she had consumed. As for her breath and why her husband didn't smell it, Jaelen, thinking ahead, had placed a Listerine strip in her mouth knowing it would dissolve.

Danna stayed in the shower for close to twenty minutes replaying her time with Jaelen, trying to hold onto to the feeling of his touch that seemed to have her melting at the tip of his fingers and tongue.

After the shower, she made her way to the kitchen past her teens' rooms, who were all on their phones and computers. For her it was like living alone, especially now knowing what her husband had been up to on his late days at work and long hours in the study. She was not stupid.

She knew what he'd been doing in the study now. At first she'd been naïve, until she witnessed firsthand his betrayal. Now all of his secrets would continue to be his own as long as she could have her life of excitement with Jaelen.

Once in the kitchen she prepared herself a grilled chicken salad as recommended by her trainer. As she exited the living room, she walked to the large window and looked out to see her car parked where it should be. Another thing Jaelen had covered. He had one of his buddies help him out with this. The thought he put into this alone made her wish she would have met him long ago, or simply wish he had been around twenty plus years ago when she had given her vows to Daniel. However, now she was accepting the path that had been paved for her and the life she was now living. No complaints about how that last few hours went. Now she was looking forward to even more excitement and the next adventure with her best-kept secret.

FOUR

8:10 p.m.

Over at Jaelen's condo, he was now joined by his two longtime friends: Lamont "Monty" Simmons, and Shawn "SK" King. Monty was twenty-six, stood five foot eleven, and weighed one hundred eighty-five fit pounds. His hair was braided, flowing with his dark close-shaven beard, black-colored eyes, and light skin, with a charming smile that lured the ladies. It also helped with his sales skills as a car dealer.

Shawn, his other buddy, was six foot even and dark-skinned, weighing one hundred ninety-six fit pounds. He loved basketball, but not as much as he loved making money off of real estate, having his own business at twenty-six.

Jaelen was coming into the living room area with beers for his buddies and an OJ and vodka for himself.

"Good looking for that save earlier with my

client's car. I don't know how she locked them in there?" Jaelen said, taking a seat with his laptop.

"I think she did it on purpose to lure you in," Monty said and then added, "especially since there weren't any keys locked inside. The only keys were the ones you gave me to drive the car."

They all laughed, but inside Jaelen's mental wheel started spinning, thinking, why would she do this? On top of that, how could she predict her husband driving past with another woman? Or was it all a coincidence that became karma on her behalf? He would have to get the truth behind this the next time they crossed paths.

"So did you put it down on her or what?" SK asked. Jaelen sipped on his drink before lowering the glass with a smirk.

"I gave her a verbal welcome into my circle of secret associates."

"That's all? I would have gave it all to her. You know I got a thing for Asian women too," SK said in between taking a gulp of his beer.

"You can't always jump on it, because if you do that and give your all, you have nothing else to prove or show them. I keep it interesting from the conversation to my touch. I want them to think about me and what's next after they leave my presence."

"Oh, you want to hypnotize the pussy?" Monty said, making them all laugh.

"Not hypnotize, mesmerize, therefore I'll always have their attention, mentally and emotionally. It's an art that comes naturally. Like an artist with a fresh canvas, each time it's going to be different, but in the end a masterpiece that can be appreciated."

"You a damn fool if you believe that shit coming out of your mouth," SK said. "There is no creature more deceptive or strategic than a woman. You think you have them all figured out and convinced with your good looks and game until you end up being the one being played."

Monty shook his head before drinking his beer, knowing what SK was saying was all but true; however, if you enter any relationship with genuine intention, you'll get the good out of it.

"All right, on to the next one. Check her out," Jaelen said, turning his laptop around displaying a photo from his client list.

"Now she's fine. I wonder how much filter she used on this picture?" SK said.

72

"None, she really looks like that in person, without makeup, all sweaty and in shape already, which keeps me intrigued about her true reason for choosing my place," Jaelen stated.

"Probably to boost her self-esteem being around fat chicks trying to get where she at," SK responded, always being brutally honest even when he shouldn't.

Monty zoomed in on the pictures, recognizing her face form television.

"You don't know who that is?" Monty asked. Each of them looked on at Monty waiting for him to tell them. "That's Anthony Falcone's wife. You know the guy who was a stockbroker, then they said he had mob ties in New York. He left the big city and moved to Mechanicsburg."

"You sure it's her? Because the last name is different," Jaelen asked.

"Punch his name in on Google along with 'wife.' I bet her picture pops up," Monty said.

Jaelen did just that only to find out his good friend was telling the truth. Her name was Laila Patrones-Falcone.

"I wonder why she didn't have this on her application for the gym or why she introduced herself as Mrs. Patrones."

"Like I said, women are the most deceptive creatures. You best believe there's a reason. The question is, at what cost are you willing to find out?"

Jaelen processing his friend's words knowing although he joked a lot speaking his mind, there was always some content and meaning behind what he spoke.

"I have to say this mysterious woman has just increased the level of intrigue, making me gravitate toward her even more."

"She has them eyes that lure you in," Monty

said. He added, "Tread with caution because we wouldn't want her husband putting a hit on you."

"Let her come to you, because it's clear there's more to her reasoning for choosing your gym when there's gyms where she lives," SK said, making Jaelen's sense of acuity heighten listening to his words of truth.

"I think that's enough for now. Let's focus on the financial aspects of our business along with the end game," he said, shutting his laptop down and becoming serious now since money was their ultimate goal and sole means for being in the business and lifestyle, they had chosen.

FIVE

9:45 a.m.

Jaelen had just finished his first class of the day and was preparing to take on his next class in fifteen minutes. All morning long he was thinking about the conversation he and his buddies had. Mainly Danna with the keys being locked in the car. Then the mysterious side Laila brought making him want to know more about her, and not just sexually. He always viewed sex as the foreplay to getting what he really wanted anyway. He also felt for him and his good looks, sex was the easiest part of it all.

As he was hydrating drinking a lemon-lime Gatorade, Danna entered the gym cheerily with a bounce in her step wearing her pink yoga pants with a tight white sports top with pink lettering that read: Body Under Construction.

Jaelen gave a brief smile reading it before coming over to address her, but first greeting her professionally.

"Good morning, Danna. Glad to see you came back to Custom Body Fitness. I take it you're looking forward to today's workout."

"Yes, I'm ready for it all," she said with a smile that was lit up with thoughts of how her workout day ended yesterday.

"Come over here. I want to point some things out to you that will help with your session today," he said, making his way over the colored dumbbells that lined the floor-to-ceiling mirrors.

"How did you get me home and fully dressed?" she asked.

"That's not important, as the 'keys locked in

the car' act you pulled on me yesterday," he responded. Her eyes locked on his, at the same time widening in surprise that he figured it out.

"Oh no. Did I just ruin all of my chances to get more of this good savory piece of chocolate?" she thought. "I'm, I'm . . ."

"You're not sorry. If you are, it means you regret what took place yesterday. My question is why? Also, was that really your husband, or was that an act too?"

Reflecting back to her husband in the car with the other female only made her become emotional as her demeanor shifted. "That was real. He came home late as if he had another day busy at work when he was probably busy fucking her."

Jaelen wanted more answers to the questions in his head. However, those questions would have to wait, since his 10:00 a.m. class was preparing to start, with his clients coming through the door.

"We'll pick this conversation up some other time. Right now, I have a class to tend to."

"Some other time like later at your place?" she asked with a soft voice and sad eyes wanting him to feel better about her, and not lack trust since he discovered her deception with the keys being locked in the car situation.

"Let's focus on the workout and let time and what's natural take its course," he said, walking away leaving her with his lingering words.

Deborah glanced up briefly, making eye contact with Jaelen and seeing the look on his face. He was in thought and allowing his thoughts to be displayed on his face. He didn't notice her looking on. However when the time was right, she would bring it up in case he needed something to be taken care of.

"Good morning, ladies," he said, welcoming

the group of women coming through the door. There were at least four new faces along with Paula and Mrs. Laila Patrones coming through the door.

"Laila, he is eye candy just as you said," said Laura Duvall, one of Laila's friends that resided in her million-dollar community in Pinehurst Estates in Mechanicsburg, Pennsylvania. Laura stood five foot one and weighed a filled-out 147 pounds. Her long, curly brown touched her shoulders. Her dimples made her look young and innocent at the age of forty-one, being a mother of two twin teenage boys.

"Yes, he is the chocolate drop you said he would be," Candice Miller added. She stood five foot three and weighed one fifty-two, placed in her hips, thighs, and large breasts. The natural redhead with light green eyes also appealed to Jaelen since they had the eye color in common. Candice, being forty-five, was the oldest of the friends, and a recently single mother of three girls ranging from twelve to twenty.

Hearing her outspoken friends blurting out their thoughts made Laila slightly embarrassed, especially as Jaelen made eye contact with her all-too-serious look as if she always meant business.

"These are my friends, Candice and Laura, who seem to be more excited about seeing you than working out," Laila said, looking at her friends that still had their eyes locked on Jaelen and his fit body that was exposed in the tight tank top he was wearing displaying his glistening biceps that were pumped up from his first session.

He appreciated the attention, especially knowing what Laila was thinking just as she was in his thoughts. He did have questions for her about the introduction of the name, but he would have to wait until later. Right now, it was time to be professional.

"I hope you ladies are ready to work your bodies today, because I have something in store to give you that burn."

"Mmmmh, I bet you can burn a lot of calories off of this frame," Candice said, getting a brief smile from him before he turned and walked to the front of the class.

Danna, hearing the women flirting with Jaelen, couldn't help but be in her emotions. She gave them the side-eye as they walk past to line up for the class. Paula, on the other hand, figured today was going to be her day to make a move on him, not these new ladies that rolled up in here as if they were the "it" girls in high school.

The class started focusing on their stomach and tightening their upper bodies while burning calories with the build and burn exercises. Jaelen also incorporated the jump rope, before lining all of the women up in front of the mirror by the dumbbell rack.

"Ladies, I want you all to take hold of two of the five-pound dumbbells. Now I want you to part your legs like this."

Hearing him say the words part your legs made Danna flash back to the shower and how he gently parted her legs working his finger and tongue magic. Danna was so caught up in her thoughts she didn't realize she was smiling with glossy eyes displaying her distance from the workout session itself, something a few of the women took notice of. They each also knew what that look and glow came from. However, they didn't know who the person behind it was.

"Ladies, as your legs are parted, I want you to lower yourselves a little," he said, coming up behind Laila and placing his hands on her hips.

"Lower a little more, please." She obliged as he continued. "Now with the dumbbells at your side, I want you to bring them up into a curl. Ten reps. You should feel your stomach clenching with each rep right here," he said, placing his hand on Laila's already tightened stomach. He was impressed. His touch made her look up at him. Not with disgust, but a level of curiosity that she would keep to herself for now. He also caught the look but kept it professional while processing his next approach to figure out more about her. He continued on, walking down the line of women guiding each of them to the burn and bodies they all desired to have. "Paula, you're killing it today going through every exercise, driven to achieve the perfection of your new body and look," he said, making her smile briefly while feeling the burn. She was going extra hard trying to get his attention, and it had worked thus far. "Ladies, staying in the squatted position, I want you to bring the dumbbells up into a shoulder press. This will tighten up those arms so when you're wearing that strapless dress, those arms will look as sexy as the dress you're wearing," he said, making the women laugh through the burning in their muscles. He came up behind Paula. "You should feel it in these areas," he said, taking both of his hands and placing them on her lats and slightly around touching the sides of her breasts, yet remaining professional. Then his hands went across her back pointing out where she should be feeling it. His hands lowered to her legs, where she was also feeling the burn from the locked-in squat position. "Are you feeling it right here too?"

"Yes, it's really burning, but it's worth the end result," she responded, breathing heavily and loving his touch on her ass, thighs, and inner thigh were the burn really could be felt.

The session continued on for ten more

minutes before their hour was up.

"That's a wrap, ladies. Give yourself a round of applause for showing up here today and working out hard to achieve your goals." They all clapped, breathing heavily and smiling, trying to look good for him at the same time. "Today we have freshly made protein cookies in three different flavors: oatmeal, peanut butter, and chocolate chip," he said, before walking over to the counter and taking his energy shake and protein cookie and taking a bite. "They are delicious," he said, wanting each of the ladies to try them.

"He can have my cookies any day of the week," Candice said to Laila and Laura.

"You can't handle a man like that. He'd have you wrapped around his finger if he simply brushed up against you by accident," Laila said, knowing how emotional her friend could be, especially having been there for her through thick and thin.

"As long as I have fun when he's doing this brushing up against me," Candice fired back as they all made their way over to the counter. Each of the ladies got their energy drinks and protein cookies.

Laila and her friends came up in the line of people preparing to exit.

"Thank you for bringing your friends along and showing them another side of fitness they'll stick to," Jaelen said. Each of them was thinking about how they would stick to him if they had a chance. Even Laila was having these thoughts, but he would never get a chance to see this, as most women easily gave into him. Besides she had a good husband. If she ventured outside of him, it would have to be worth it, but for now the thoughts of having fun with Jaelen would do.

"We all needed a workout like this to get

ourselves fit for the summer," Laila said.

"It's also a way to lower and release some stress that could be built up."

"I could think of other stress relievers too," Candice said. Laura bumped her with her arm, shaking her head. Jaelen, on the other hand, instead of responding to her, took a bite of his protein cookie. Laila took notice of his speechless moment. She also noticed the crumbs on his face around his mouth from the cookie. Instinctively she reached up and wiped the corner of his mouth. It wasn't thought out or planned. It just happened. It caught him off guard; however, he didn't resist her touch or caring gesture. Still in the motion of wiping his face, she realized what she just did, something she would normally do to her husband when they were sharing a meal together.

"Take your time to enjoy the cookie. It's yours; no one is going to take it away from you," she said, using metaphor to tweak his curiosity even more. Her words were sent as her hand came off of his face. He appreciated her touch. He wanted more. He wanted her sexual cookies to be his as she seemed to hint. As these thoughts entered his mind, he caught the look on Danna's face, along with Paula, who both were waiting to see him off until the next session.

Laila regained herself, being a lady of class. Her smile faded as she took a sip of her chocolate energy shake.

"This chocolate with a hint of vanilla is really good," she said, walking away. Her friends followed as they eyed Jaelen up and down, taking him in visually until the next time they would see him, if they were not too sore in the morning.

Danna started her way up toward Jaelen

wondering if she was going to be able to have some of him and his time today before her husband got off work. Each step she took closing in on him, her heart beat faster, turned on by her thoughts. She could let him take her now any way he liked, even on the couch by the door for customers waiting to fill out applications.

As soon as she took another step, she lit up smiling, ready to be in his presence, when her smile shifted seeing her husband coming through the door with a box of food from the Healthy Kitchen restaurant.

"Danna, my love," he said with a smile. He was only here to make up for missing her calls yesterday. She made her way over to him, now forcing her smile as if she was happy to see him. "I brought some food as prescribed on your diet plan," he said, handing it to her before pulling her in for a kiss. Then he stepped back taking a look at her. "You look good, my love," he added, trying to play up to her. They exited together, leaving the other females to speak to Jaelen, asking workout and diet questions to find a better version of themselves.

Paula was in the midst of these women

tossing her questions and looks at him getting his attention. He held his finger up to her wanting her to stick around a little longer. She did just that, appeased that she finally got his attention to have some of his time without all of the other women gawking for his time and space.

"Paula, how's it going?" he asked, staying professional and walking over by the heavy bags where his next class would take place.

"I'm doing just fine. I wish I had a workout plan to make my long-time fiancé get on the same wave as me, but that's another topic," she said, placing her hands on her hips giving him a visual of her God-given curves that were strategically placed. Her diamond engagement ring sparkled, but she was as lonely as the solitary stone. He could see it in her eyes and demeanor.

"I don't usually venture into my clients' personal lives outside of their diets and workouts, but I see you don't have a bunch of friends to talk to like the other women," he said, looking on at her in between placing the boxing gloves by each bag. "What do you value more? Him and his time? Or yourself and your true worth?"

She folded her arms, not to be closed off, but to process the question. Her eyebrows also raised trying to figure out if this was one of those trick questions. It wasn't. The answer was whatever she believed was true to fit her and the life she desired.

"I love him, and I love me too. I guess I value what we have."

Hearing her response only allowed him to know she really had no clue. She needed direction.

"Your answer is your own thoughts and

feelings. However, you're more in love with the American way and idea of the engagement process and all that comes with it. If you loved yourself as much as you loved the idea of being married, you may already have what you want. Then again, if you love him and how he's treating you, then you're right where you want to be in life."

She unfolded her arms, taken back by his truth that made her realize the situation she was in.

Her eyes became vitreous thinking about the relationship she was in. A three-year engagement was truly a waste of time. It was like the rabbit chasing the carrot on a string.

"I guess I'm the rabbit in this situation," she said. Jaelen looked up from placing the gloves on the floor, seeing that her eyes were flooding with emotional tears. He wanted to comfort her the best he could professionally, since he had invited this conversation that led outside of working out.

"You're one sexy rabbit if that's how you want to look at it," he said, making her laugh lightly as she wiped the corners of her eyes. He took hold of his towel, coming close to her assisting her in wiping away her tears. "Pain means that emotional or physical is weakness leaving the body. Once you have time to really think over the direction you want to go in life, the pain will dissipate, unless you find a balance to this unwieldy situation you're in."

She heard his words and at the same time embraced his genuine caring touch. Paula leaned in, pulling him close and hugging him as she buried her head into his chest. Jaelen looked over at Deborah, who was looking back at him shaking her head. Not because of him but these women that would do anything for his attention.

Paula could feel his masculine chest on her face and tight abs with a chiseled six-pack against her body. Her fiancé didn't have this. In fact, he didn't even work out.

"Paula, I have a class preparing to come in. You can stick around if you want to continue talking, or I can call you later if you like, if you still need someone to talk to, to vent your thoughts to or to give you advice."

She released her embrace and stepped back looking up at him.

"I'll be fine. I think when I go home, I'll speak

my mind to him to see where he really wants to take this relationship."

"Good luck on your emotional journey. In the event something comes up, you have my social media info. Be good to yourself and always know your true worth, Paula," he said as she walked away, rushing out to her car feeling emotional. This was partly because she was having thoughts of Jaelen when she realized she hadn't felt this fire in her belly since the first year of her relationship with her fiancé. The excitement that came over her when he wiped her tears away, leading to the embrace, and feeling his firm body up against hers had a stream of butterflies fluttering inside of her. This feeling made her feel guilty, because it was what she should be feeling with her man. At the same time, now she knew if it didn't happen with her man, she had someone to call on.

SIX

3:15 p.m.

Jaelen was closing up the gym making his way over to his truck when he found a note slipped under his windshield wiper. This intrigued him, and he wanted to know who it was from. He took hold of it, at the same time scanning the cars in the parking lot making sure he wasn't being watched. He opened up the folded note that read: "The look in your eyes speaks to me. Your body lures me in. Your touch gives me an erotic rush that stimulates sinful thoughts and lust."

He finished reading the note and looked around once more smiling, wishing to see the author of this brief note that intrigued him. He jumped into his truck and turned the music on, still smiling and trying to figure out who would leave this on his car. He didn't recognize the handwriting, and the author didn't sign it. He knew he couldn't just ask around because that would make him look like he got around, when

he genuinely liked to choose his intimate circle

of secret friends. He placed the note on the

passenger seat as he backed out of his parking

space. He didn't realize he was being watched.

An admirer? A client? Ex-lover? Any relation to

the note? He would soon find out.

Jaelen headed to the grocery store to get a

few things he needed for his meal, along with

some fresh fruits for his shake he liked to make.

As he was driving there was a car four cars

back tailing him. Wanting to get close to him.

Wanting to see where he was going. To see who

he was doing, if anyone at all. He didn't pay anyone any mind, being focused on the road in front of him. At the same time he processed his thoughts on his day thus far and what was needed to be done throughout the rest of the day. This was how his mind worked: nonstop until he fell asleep. He always wanted to be a step ahead in business as well as in life. This trait gave him comfort, like a chess player who knew his next few moves before their opponent even moved.

It didn't take long before he made it to Wegmans grocery store in Camp Hill. It boasted the best brands that are fresh, being brought in daily.

He parked his truck before jumping out, still unaware he was being watched. They wanted to be inside of his head knowing his every move. Inside his most intimate thoughts so they could know what made him who he was.

Jaelen was always in business mode, but he saw women looking at him as he was passing by. So he took the time to shout out his gym's name.

"Custom Body Fitness.com. Look me up to get your fitness fix," he said, getting smiles from the women passing by. He entered the store and headed to the fresh fruits and vegetables aisle. He already knew what he wanted, so it wouldn't take long. He grabbed a few pounds of strawberries; red, purple, and green grapes, bananas, kiwis, mangos, and tangerines. Then he headed further down, getting fresh romaine and iceberg lettuce, with cherry tomatoes and more. He was focused on his meal tonight along with his daily eating habits.

He moved through the store and got his angel hair pasta for his spaghetti pie he loved to make. He made the sauce from scratch as taught to him by one of his older lady friends he associated with years ago.

As he walked through the aisle toward the end, now finished getting what he had come for, a female turned the corner with her cart, getting his attention immediately since she almost ran him over seeming to be in a rush. He extended his hand, holding the basket in the other hand.

"Oh, I'm sorry, sir," she said.

Right then Jaelen's eyes went from the end of the cart that almost hit him, up to the female apologizing, and instantly saw Laila Patrones-Falcone. His heart jumped wondering how convenient this was. At that same time he flashed back to the note left on his truck. "Damn, it would be nice if it was her," he thought.

"Sir, coming from the women who got on me about calling her ma'am?"

"I'm sorry, Jaelen. I didn't realize I almost ran over my favorite fitness instructor."

"So, you have other instructors I'm in competition with?" he asked being funny.

She smiled, lighting up. "No, no, you're the only one who has my body's attention," she responded, tweaking his mental curiosity about this meeting with her in the store.

His heart felt her words at the same time his mind processed the last sentence of him having her body's attention.

This only made him want her even more.

He was looking into her cart seeing the items she had already.

"It's good to see you're sticking to the diet plan," he said, then added, "How are the recipes coming along. Are they tasty enough for you?"

"They would be if I knew how to cook as good as the pictures you have of these meals on your website," she said. He laughed lightly.

"It would be my pleasure to show you how to

cook a perfect meal that will appease your taste buds and body," he said with hopes of getting her to bite on the concept of him cooking her a meal. A smirk came across her face before licking her lips in a salacious manner.

"So let me guess how this is going to play out: dinner at your place, wine of course, then dessert chocolate perhaps?" she said, looking at him up and down. He could feel his body heating up as he was getting closer to luring her in. It was a rush kind of like a hunter closing in on its prey, finger in the trigger guard, breathing picking up, eye on the scope on the prey that was about to meet its fate. However, in this case, her fate would be euphoric, satisfying her every desire.

He reached into his basket taking out a strawberry.

"You have a creative imagination. You can make this disappear with a little magic, and blindfolded I could find it," he said, using metaphors before taking a bite of the strawberry, seeing her lured into his lyrical grasp as she was visualizing the places she would make it vanish with him discovering it and every part of her body. Lost in her thoughts she didn't even realize her lips were parted sucking in a heated breath. Butterflies raced through her before she took control, pulling herself together, closing her mouth, and giving him a sneer and side-eye.

"I'll figure this cooking thing out as I always do. Nice seeing you," she said, shifting her cart to pass him. Seeing this he started feeling this neurotic sensation as if he was about to allow this opportunity to slip away. As the cart started past him, he halted it, placing his hand on top of hers. Masculine, yet a gentle, calm stimulation that made her take in a heated breath looking down at his hand then back up to him. He could see something in her eyes that made him gravitate toward her close enough for a kiss, but he halted himself, taking in her floral perfume scent. She could now feel the heat of his breath close to her face that slid close to her neck up to her ear.

"When you're truly ready to leap into the fire of passion that's burning inside of you, I'll be there to welcome you, appeasing your every desire," he said before walking away, vanishing into the store leaving her to think of his words and touch. She was stuck in the middle of the aisle, looking back to see if he was around, but nothing. He was physically gone, but mentally lingering around in her thoughts.

Laila gave a light laugh, exhaling before proceeding with her grocery shopping.

Jaelen exited the store with his groceries smiling as he was thinking about his approach. He figured Laila was either on the fence with him or she was that good at playing the game. Either way, he too stepped his game up, being strategic to lure her in.

As he was making his way over to the truck, he noticed a female in the front by the driver's side placing something on the windshield. His

smile faded as he rushed over to his truck.

"Excuse me, ma'am, what are you doing?"

he asked, reflecting back to the first note. Was

she the one who placed the first note? When

she turned to face him, he recognized that she

was one of his clients from the afternoon class.

"Tanya, what is that?" he asked, sitting his

groceries down before taking the note from

under his windshield wiper.

As he started unfolding the note, she started

speaking, trying to plea her case.

"I didn't know how to tell you or talk to you

the way the other women do. I figured they're married and I'm single; I should have a better chance than they do," she blurted, looking up at him as he unfolded the note.

It read: "I would give you the world if you gave me the time, your touch and all every day."

Tanya Moss a full-figured blond, stood five foot six and weighed 161 pounds. She was only twenty-nine years old, with no kids, and was single with baby-blue eyes. She was picturesque smiling with her white teeth. Tanya was from Hershey, Pennsylvania, which was less than twenty minutes from the gym in

Harrisburg. She came from a wealthy family that was respected in Hershey and the prestigious gated community they lived in. Tanya didn't flaunt her wealth because she wanted a man to like, love, and appreciate her for who she was inside and out.

"I assume the other note was from you too?" he asked, picking the basket up and placing his things in the back seat before setting the basket with the other on the aisle by the lamp post.

"Yes, I just wanted to get your attention. I wanted you to see me as you do the others."

"I see everyone, Tanya. Each female in my

classes can say they have had my up-close attention, because I want to work with my clients so they can build their confidence and feel comfortable working out," he said, closing the back door on the truck. "You have my attention outside of the gym. Now what would you like?" he asked, catching her off guard. She hadn't thought this through. She figured leaving the notes behind would add intrigue, leading up to her great reveal. However, now that wasn't the case; what she'd been wanting was right here before her.

"I, I want you. I want to be in your space, to

talk to you and laugh with you outside of the gym." She paused, allowing him to absorb her words. He was looking back on at her wearing the YSL jeans that were hugging her thick thighs, the white Vera Wang top with white flats. Her hair was down, unlike how she wore it at the gym. Her natural look was sexy yet different from the others he encountered. Her lips were full and glossy. He could tell she was the shy type and used to be bigger, but now with her fit thickness she was trying to gain her confidence and build her self-esteem by coming to his gym in search of a new refined body.

"This is what I want you to do, Tanya: get in your car and follow me. I'm on my way home to shower and make something to eat. You can join me for dinner and make this our first date." Hearing him say this, she lit up like a Las Vegas light bulb.

"Okay, okay. My car is over there. Thank you," she said, turning and rushing over to her car. She didn't realize Jaelen had had his eye on her for other reasons. He just hadn't known she would come off to him as she had. She did the groundwork for him, placing herself in his mental, physical, and emotional grasp. He smiled as he pulled off, making a call to his buddy, Monty. He picked up on the second ring.

"What's going on, Jaelen?" Monty asked.

"I'm going to be using the crib with this blond bombshell, feel me?" he said. Monty already knew who he was talking about, no names needed. They had codes for each of the women.

"You rushing to it, huh?" he said, knowing Jaelen was ahead of schedule with Tanya. She'd been at the gym for a month now.

"Wait until I tell you how it all came together. I started feeling like I was being lured into a situation."

Monty started laughing knowing how his best friend thought.

"Keep me in the loop," Monty said, then added, "Don't destroy anything."

"You know that wasn't me last time; that was the crazy lady I was with. Don't worry, I got this over here."

He hung up the phone and made his way to Forest Hills Estate on the edge of Harrisburg. Monty had a five thousand-square-foot property fully furnished with all of the bachelor amenities. He used it when he could, since he had multiple properties in this state and up and down the

East Coast that he rented out as time shares for

added income.

SEVEN

Jaelen and Tanya were pulling up into the driveway of the four-car-garage home, boasting dual fireplaces inside, and one by the pool for winter nights in the hot tub. There wouldn't be any need for these amenities tonight, only Jaelen's God-given talents, physically and lyrically.

"This is a nice place you have," Tanya said.

"It serves its purpose," Jaelen responded, not wanting to make her aware that it was his friend's place. She would never know since there weren't any personal photos in this home, only expensive pieces of art framed and placed around the home to Monty's liking.

As they entered the home Tanya started feeling good, finally being able to capture his attention as she had fantasized about, since he never seemed to give her the attention she yearned for in his classes.

"Take a seat over there. Make yourself at

home. What would you like to drink?"

"A glass of wine would be fine," she responded.

"Red or white?"

"Surprise me," she responded with a smile and eyes full of lust wanting to pour the wine over his body and sip each drop. At least this would be her fantasy, not that he would take it past that.

He exited, making his way into the kitchen and placing the food on the countertop. Then he made his way over to the temperature-controlled wine cabinet with a glass door allowing one to view every selection before opening the door. The bottles in it ranged from $40 to L`Esprit de Tiffon, which was $19k per bottle. He smiled thinking about choosing that bottle. It was also a choice he would share with Laila, but now was not her time. This evening was about Tanya getting her fantasy fulfilled, or at least she would come close to it. Since he was not one for giving it all to them at once.

He took hold of a bottle of Laubade 1961, a $376 bottle. He made his way to the cabinet and took out two glasses, pouring some for her and him. He made his way into the living room, where he discovered her standing taking in all of the art.

"I see you have a taste for art," he said as he made his way over to her and extended the glass of wine. She took the glass smiling. She'd waited a long time to be in his presence.

"To a good evening," she said, toasting her glass with his before taking a sip. "Mmmh, good choice: 1961 Laubade," she added. It impressed him that she knew her wine and also had a great appreciation for art.

"So, what do you know and like about the art you see?" he asked.

"I'm curious to know if the abstract expression 'Asheville' 1948 by Wilen de Kooning is real along with the action painting 'United Ink' on paper, by Jackson Pollock 1950, because last I checked the Museum of Modern Art was the home of these fine pieces."

"Whether they've found a new home or not, it's to be appreciated," he responded, evading the question.

"What about the Akhenaton head sculpture? That looks like the real thing too. The question would be, who sold such timeless pieces?"

He understood she had a great love for the

arts and finer things. However, her questioning the origins of these authentic pieces of art wasn't good, so he took control of the situation.

"Can you imagine the two of us body painting creating our own art that could possibly be timeless pieces?" he said, stepping close to her. She lowered her glass of wine welcoming the closeness. He took his free hand and caressed her hair over her ear. His touch was stimulating, and her eyes locked on him wanting more, yet strangely wanting to resist to also be a lady. "Your face, lips, and perfect dimples make God the greatest artist of all times." She let out light laughter, smiling and still welcoming his touch.

His hand went under her chin and raised it as he

closed in inches away from her flushed lips.

"You're a masterpiece waiting to be discovered,"

he said, pulling back from what she thought was

going to be a passionate kiss. "Now let me get

cleaned up so I can cook this food for us."

"How about you shower, and I order

something for us, so you don't have to waste

time in the kitchen?" she suggested, wanting to

cut to the chase of him being in the kitchen for

more than an hour, when that hour could be

spent with her.

"Sounds like a plan. If you need any more wine, it's on the counter in the kitchen," he said, drinking the wine and placing it on the counter as he passed through before heading up to the master bedroom to shower. He and Monty kept clothes here, since they all wore the same sizes other than shoes and sneakers. It didn't matter anyway; everything was brand new. As Jaelen left Tanya alone, she took in a breath before gulping her wine, something she would never do being ladylike, but she needed to calm herself down after that heated encounter. She headed into the kitchen, found the bottle, and poured another glass before placing a call to order sushi for the two of them. This was somewhat healthy, and he hadn't specified what he wanted.

Within thirty minutes, Jaelen came into the living room wearing navy blue silk pajama pants with a robe to match. What really caught Tanya's eye was the partially open robe displaying a glimpse of his glistening chest and chiseled six-pack. She zoomed in sipping on her wine and allowing her mind to take her the rest of the way.

"So, what did you order?" he asked, taking a seat beside her.

"A variety of sushi, if you don't mind?"

"Good choice. You can never go wrong with sushi, in my eyes," he said, taking a pair of chopsticks preparing to eat, until she took charge feeding him. This caught him by surprise as he bit into the sushi. The feeling she was having right in this moment comforted her as if they'd been together for some time. It also made every decision she made feel effortless.

They enjoyed each other's company as well as the sushi. Conversation flowed, just as her eyes over him each time he got up to get more wine, since they had consumed the first bottle. Jaelen turned the music on playing Tre Songz's

Billboard hit album. Another of her favorites, being a fan of his for some time. Now she was a fan of Jaelen's sexy body she could now see as he slipped the robe off and placed it on the arm of the couch. She was wanting to reach out and allow her hands to roam over his body. Be a good girl, Tanya, she thought, coaching herself and feeling the buzz of the wine.

"Tanya, you want my attention, and you got it. Now I want to show you how much I appreciate your boldness coming onto me as you did," he said moving closer to her. "Let me see your feet," he said. She obliged, taking her shoes off one by one. He started massaging her foot. His touch melted her. "You like how this feels?" he asked. She nodded in between sipping her wine. "Are you comfortable with your new body yet?" he asked, wanting to know if she would be willing to go further. She understood clearly what he wanted.

"Yes, depending on who I'm around."

"No, of course. The one who assisted you in achieving this art I view as perfection," he said, sending his words with a smile. Not that he had to; she was all his at this point. The wine only allowed her to open up, wanting him even more.

"I'm going to massage your body from head to toe," he said. He came up and placed a kiss on her neck, then her shoulder as his fingers caressed her breasts before making their way down to her pants, unbuttoning them and removing her from her clothing. She came out of the top as he removed the pants, leaving her in the powder-blue panty and bra set. He placed her left leg up on his shoulder as he began his massage, working his fingers deep into her calves, then up to her thighs. She let out a sensual moan enjoying this massage. He switched legs, tending to the other before lying her legs side by side and pressing down, massaging each thigh at the same time. "Finish up your wine; I want you to turn over." She did just that, turning over on her belly. He turned around to his robe, removing the vanilla-scented massage oil in a small four-ounce bottle. He allowed the oil to drip over her back and legs. The coolness of the oil felt good to her. As he began to massage her body, the oil seemed to heat up to the right temperature, stimulating her body. His hand and fingers pressed deep down her back over her bottom, going on the outside of her panties. His fingers slipped under her panties, massaging her bottom down to the middle of her thighs, close to her area of passion. Her heart and mind were racing, loving his touch. He leaned in close, allowing his breathing to be felt over her legs up to her bottom, where he continued pressing his fingers and hands deep. At the same time he parted her cheeks, allowing his fingers to flow over her down to her now heated and wet passion spot. He stayed away from creating even more desire for her to want him. His breathing now could be felt in between her legs inches away from her love spot. Her breathing was picking up, never having this done before. No one had ever wanted to massage her body, let alone become this intimate in massaging her. She could feel her stomach fluttering with butterflies trying to anticipate how this was going to end. She no longer wanted to masturbate for pleasure thinking about him; she wanted the real thing. Her mouth was open panting for his touch. As he was taking each breath, she could feel it between her thighs close to her V. His fingers moved closer, just as his lips closed in on her cheeks, placing a kiss to them before pulling back, continuing his massage. He went up over her back and then her shoulders before he leaned over to her ear.

"Is this the attention you desired from me?"

he whispered into her ear. She let out a light moan and laughter.

"You're bad in a good way. This is more than I imagined."

"The best is coming. Look, don't touch; touch, don't taste; taste, don't swallow. How much control do you have over your desires?" he asked, sliding his fingers over her back and bottom into her panties, finding her soft, wet, and warm playground. She moaned, and his thick finger parted her, entering slow with pressure.

"Mmmmh, mmmmh. This is good, mmmmh."

"Now imagine feeling this good and resisting the orgasm, holding it back until you can't hold it anymore," he whispered into her ear as his fingers continued to press deep into her body creating a surging pulsating feeling bouncing around inside of her as she was trying to hold it back. This powerful feeling that was building up forced her moans and breathing to become heavier and louder.

"Mmmmmh. Ooooh God, oooooh God, mmmmmmh." He started going faster and faster while coaching her.

"Hold it back, even if you have to squeeze

my fingers to embrace the intense feeling." Her breathing became intense as her hands took hold of the pillow, pulling it close and squeezing it as her bottom was backing into his fingers, squeezing her vagina on him. This only created another surging wave of orgasms that wanted to be released.

"Oooooh God, mmmmmmmh, mmmmh. Ooooh my God, ooooh God, mmmmmmmmh." She let out now, unable to hold it back, feeling her stomach clenching and her legs shaking. "Oooh God, I can't, I can't hold it back anymore, mmmmmh, mmmmm," she let out as the powerful buildup of pleasure took over her body,

escaping at a pulsating rate. Her moans turned

to heavy breathing, and her stomach tightened

as her legs trembled in between her backing into

his fingers until that too came to a halt as the

ultimate climax came, holding her in place. He

held his fingers still, feeling her vagina

contracting over and over as it released

powerful waves of orgasms. Her warmth and

wetness were more than he'd ever experienced,

as if she'd been neglected by the touch of a man

for quite some time. He leaned in, placing his

lips on her bottom and kissing it softly, making

her feel even more pleasure she didn't think

could be felt. His kisses turning into an erotic love bite made her moan. "Ooooh, mmmmmh." He removed his fingers and placed them to his nose, closing his eyes and taking in her sweet scent, before caressing his lips with her juices. "She's special," he thought. "Special for many reasons."

He raised up from his love bites and allowed his kisses to trail up her spine until he reached her neck, then the side of her faces that was pressing against the pillow she was holding tight.

"I'm glad you took the time to get my

attention," he whispered, placing a kiss to her face. "This is just the beginning of what's to come."

Her eyes were still closed, and she felt good hearing his words accompanied by the orgasmic rush that had calmed her desires for him. She wanted him inside of her, so she could wrap her arms and legs around him and hold onto him. She turned over, opening her eyes and facing him.

"I want you to be good to me and my body," she said, kissing his lips. For the first time he could feel the passion in her kiss. Normally he would be the one in control, but this kiss seemed to control him. He enjoyed it but didn't want to be taken by this moment he knew felt so right. He pulled back from the passionate kiss.

"Let's take it slow, enjoying the time we have together and knowing that each time we do come together, it will be as explosive as this." He took her hand and guided it to his masculine chest, caressing it before leading her down to his cut six-pack. She giggled at the touch of his in-shape body. She'd never been with anyone who was as fit as he was. In fact, she'd only been with two other guys in her entire life since she used to be heavier growing up. Her hand slid from his, going down further and caressing the outside of his silk pajamas, feeling his length and thickness. She let out a moan, turned on feeling the power of passion holding onto him.

"Mmmmmh, I'm looking forward to meeting you," she said, looking at his manhood. This made him laugh as he moved her hand away.

"Sex is best when we make it interesting. Tonight is the first step of foreplay that will make you and I come back for more. We know what we have, yet we can't have it as we please. It's a slight tease, keeping it interesting and stimulating our hearts, minds and bodies along

the way," he said, raising her leg up and placing

a kiss on it before massaging her calf. "Your

body is art in itself to be valued and fully

appreciated, because what you have is precious

and priceless," he added, placing more kisses to

her legs and down into between her thighs,

making her feel as if this was about to happen,

his tongue on her body, or him parting her legs

to take her in the most intimate way. He closed

in on her place of passion, placing a kiss on it

that she could feel even though it was through

her panties. A light moan escaped her mouth.

He came up looking on at her and saw the lust

and stimulation in her eyes and on her face. "This is the art worth waiting to appreciate."

"No, no, don't tease me like this," she thought as she smiled back at him. He leaned back still having her leg on his lap massaging her feet as they continued to talk about what she really wanted from him, as well as the promises he was willing to make to her and for her. This was something he didn't normally do. However, she was different. Her difference motivated his true means of wanting to get to know more about her and what made her smile inside and out. What made her tick and look forward to each day? The evening turned to night as the conversation, drinking, and laughter turned to cuddling, comfort, and deep sleep as she lay her head on his chest, feeling its warmth and firmness, which placed her at ease. He allowed this, since he knew she was going to be worth it in the long run. Other women would be long gone or on their way home by now, but Tanya, she could stay, not realizing how special and unique this very moment lying with him was.

EIGHT

The next day Jaelen was conducting business as usual, teaching his classes and encouraging women to achieve their perfection. He noticed today Danna wasn't as forward as she was the day before wanting his attention. He could see it in her eyes that there was something she was keeping from him. He wanted to know what it was. He also noticed that Laila didn't show up, but her girlfriends were present loving every bit of being present and taking in the eye candy that Jaelen was to them. The class, having less than twenty minutes remaining when Paula rolled in late, seeming distraught. This, too, piqued his curiosity, making him want to know why she was late and coming in with a look on her face as if she was yearning for attention and may be neglected.

Jaelen, in the midst of his day thus far, was also flashing back to his good night with Tanya, followed by the breakfast she cooked when she woke up before him. Breakfast was followed by the kisses she wanted so bad to let her know that she wasn't dreaming about his touch last night. After breakfast they showered, keeping their distance and not touching one another as he requested yet taking in the art of each other's beauty. She wanted all of his bare muscular flesh that she witnessed. She wanted to wash him just to be close, but he didn't allow it. "Look, don't touch," he reminded her. She obliged yet wanted more, more that she was going to be looking forward to today after her session with him.

The class came to an end with his clients jumping rope for the last five minutes. He was also jumping rope for the last five minutes, counting down the minutes, allowing the women to know how close they were to completion.

"Last minute, ladies. You're looking good. Working out is the hard part. Looking good as a result of working out is the easy part," he said, sweating more than usual since he drank a lot of water this morning to hydrate after his night of wine exploration with Tanya. "Time, ladies. You should all be proud of yourselves for coming another day. This makes you all a step closer to achieving that custom fit body that will make your boyfriends, husbands, fiancés, and lovers gravitate toward you even more," he said, flipping the rope over his shoulder before wiping his forehead. "Today we have fudge brownie protein bars along with drinks to hydrate, so you ladies can keep your skin right and glowing," he said, making his way over to the door to see his clients off as always, keeping it formal. He noticed Paula wasn't in line; she was over by the mirrored wall stretching, touching her toes before placing her hands flat on the ground in front of her. Candice and Laura were happy to see Jaelen again.

"Thank you, Mr. Chocolate Drop, for working our bodies to perfection," Candice said. Laura shook her head as if she was embarrassed. "What? I'm only saying what you and Laila be thinking and talking about." Now Laura really turned red in the face, clearly exposed. Jaelen was surprised that he was even a topic of conversation amongst the three friends.

"Where is Laila today?" he asked, missing seeing her and at the same time missing their scintillating encounters that had him wanting to know more about her. She had him feeling a need to chase, although he had resisted it yesterday.

"She had to drive her husband to the airport for his business trip to Tokyo," Laura said, sliding the fudge brownie over her lips before biting into it. For some strange reason Jaelen caught what she was doing but tried to act as if he didn't see it. Right now, he had his plate full trying to stay ahead and afloat with what he had going on.

"Hopefully she can join us tomorrow. Let her know she missed out on a good workout today."

"She missed more than that with you bouncing up and down," Candice said, giving a quick glance below Jaelen's waist. She was referring to the jump rope and jumping jacks that made his private parts protrude, catching their attention each time he was jumping up and down. This wasn't done on purpose, and he would take care of it by wearing a jockstrap in the future.

The ladies exited along with the rest of the class. Even Danna continued walking until he Jaelen halted her.

"In a hurry or worn out from the workout?" he asked, trying to feel her out. She shook her head as she responded.

"I thank you for being nice to me, but yesterday when my husband came in, I resisted him, until we started talking and being honest."

"Let's step outside real quick," he said, knowing this conversation wasn't for anyone inside. She followed. Normally he wouldn't care about what she thought or felt, but she was now a part of his plan. His end game. He also viewed her as someone he could have fun with. "Help me understand what you're saying."

"I told him I know about the girl. I didn't tell him about us or what happened, but he assumed something. I have a family."

"You also had fun yesterday. I allowed you to escape to a place where pain, the pain you were feeling, didn't exist."

He paused, allowing his words to reach out to her. He needed her to be on the same page, because if she left the gym today, she may never show back up after making this moment awkward. "Close your eyes, Danna." She obliged. "Find me in the shower as you boldly did. Feel my touch, the rush, the excitement that took over your body, heart, and mind in that very moment. How did you feel? If you could, would you have more of that moment in the shower?"

Her eyes still closed and her breathing picked up as she vividly placed herself into that moment.

"I want more," she let out, at the same time opening her eyes as if she didn't have control over the words coming out of her mouth. A brief smile came to her face before she turned to leave, leaving him confused and wondering if he had ruined his chances with her and the opportunity to have her around. He turned to head back into the gym and walked past Deborah.

"You're losing your touch, Jae. Pull it

together," she said. He respected her words and opinion always, so he didn't mind when she pulled him up or brought something to his attention. She always had his best interest in mind. "Jae, you also have a private appointment that just came in. They're also paying double the asking fee to make them a priority." She slid the info across the counter. He took hold of it. He didn't even look at it because he was focused on keeping things in line as planned. He placed the paper into his gym bag before making his way over the Paula.

"How's it going, Paula?"

"I got a slow start to my day no thanks to my now ex-fiancé, that cheating bastard. I can't even be that mad. I should have seen this coming a mile away, especially with how long I've had that ring."

"Had?"

"Yeah, I flushed that shit down the toilet, because seeing the women in his phone and the messages back and forth devalued what I believed we had."

"I'm normally a man of many word, but I'll allow my workout to be your therapy today. So you can stay for this next class to release that anger and stress you're feeling. We're going to be hitting the bags today in my next class," he said. At the same time, his clients started filtering in.

Paula was definitely in need of venting the emotions she'd allowed to build up overnight until she cried herself to sleep at the hotel she stayed in last night, wanting to be far away from her fiancé as possible.

The class started with stretching followed by jumping jacks to warm up. Then they transitioned over to the heavy bags. Jaelen secured the twelve-ounce bag gloves onto each client before starting the time. He coached them along the way.

"Remember the one person that didn't think you could do this? Yeah, that's their face you're crashing into. That guy that didn't look at you but wants you in his life right now. Yeah, this is for him. Punch the pounds off, ladies. At the same time let the frustration and pain out. Don't let it hold you down any longer," he instructed. The ladies started punching the bag harder and faster, some letting out light screams as they were talking to the bags and punching them visualizing the faces of the ones who had angered them. Paula was sweating heavily and tears were streaming down her face as she continued slamming her fists into the bag thinking about how she had been betrayed. Jaelen could see this. A part of him wanted to step in to help her, but she needed this. She needed to get it all out to feel better. Then he could make his move.

Close to forty-five minutes had passed. The class came to an end with the women breathing heavily and sweating more than they ever had. At the same time they felt renewed, having unleashed the buildup of anger and emotions by punching the bag.

"I really needed that," the dark chocolate Afro-American female said with her skin glistening as if she had just come off the set of Black Panther. Jaelen always noticed her, but kept it professional, because she wasn't a part of his plan or end game.

"I got a lot of built-up emotions and frustrations out that seemed to be weighing me down," Paula let out, agreeing with the other female.

The class came to an end. It was a short day for Jaelen, and Deborah also made her way out, reminding him not to forget his private session that was paying double.

Jaelen noticed that Paula was still over by the heavy bags. He couldn't figure her out, or her approach, but right now he would have to think this through knowing she was emotional. He locked the door to the gym and made his way over to her, taking a seat on the bench beside her.

"What are you doing here, Paula?"

She turned to face him, looking into his eyes. Her eyes weren't sad as they were when she entered today. There was something intriguing behind them. He needed to find out what exactly it was.

"I'm valuing my true worth, being in your presence. I'm in control of my own destiny."

"It sounds like you want me to take control to guide you in the direction you truly desire to be," he said, standing up and taking her hand. She didn't resist. She followed him over to the corner, out of sight of people passing by, yet they could see out if they chose. He led her to the dip and pull-up bars. The medicine balls and large to small exercise balls were also over in this corner. "Stand in between the dip bar," he said taking hold of a pair of hand wraps and coming back over to her. "Are you ready to escape to your place of destiny, a place where emotional heartache and pain doesn't exist?"

She shook her head yes, looking into his eyes slightly in fear of what was next. A part of her was asking, "What did I get myself into?"

He started securing her hand to the cool steel dip bar. "Keep your hand flat, holding onto the bar," he said, knowing the simulation of the thick bar would also enhance her thoughts and emotions, teasing her body when it all came together.

Once both hands were secured, he walked around to the back of her and slid his hand up her sweaty back raising her shirt up a little. Then his hands came back down to her waistline pulling her yoga pants down exposing her curves of perfection that didn't budge as he continued to remove her pants down to her feet, allowing her to step out of them. He placed them to his nose taking in her sweet sweat, before he tossed them to the side. His creative yet spontaneous genius kicked in, and he took two jump ropes that were outfitted with plastic smooth casings and closed in on her, going underneath her, caressing her V before taking hold of each rope and crisscrossing them to have an effect on her each time she moved as he instructed. The ropes made an X on her V as they came up over her breasts, pressing down on them, turning her on even more the tighter he secured them. Her body heated up as she moved slightly trying to adjust herself only to trigger the motion of the ropes pressing perfectly up against her pearl, massaging it in each direction up and down. A part of her let out a light giggle wondering how she allowed this to happen, yet blown away by the position knowing more was to come.

"Are you comfortable?"

"Yes," she responded, turning her head to get a glimpse of him behind her, wondering what was next.

"How could one stray away from such greatness?" he said, placing his lips against her sweet sweaty neck. Her head leaned back as his hands came around to her breasts, pressing up against them and making the ropes tighten, placing pressure on her pearl as he gently squeezed her breasts, stimulating her from each angle. His fingers let up as she let out a sigh of passion. He took the rope and tugged at it lightly.

"Aaaah, this is so wrong, but good," she let out, feeling her body heating up. His free hand pressed up against the small of her back to keep her strategically placed where the pressure of the ropes would massage her pearl. He tugged at the rope again, creating a rushing feeling as her pearl was locked between the smooth plastic of the ropes. "Aaaaah, aaaaah, aaaah," she moaned with her head back. He let go of her only to drop his shorts exposing all of his thickness and length. Then he took hold of a five-pound medicine ball and lowered himself down, parting her legs and extending the cantaloupe-sized ball out to her knees.

"Close your legs to hold this place, until I say let it go." She did as she was told only to feel a orgasmic surge in closing her legs, pressing up even more on her pearl that was pulsating and now super sensitive. A light wind could blow and make her moan.

"Aaaah, what's happening to me? Aaah," she let out as her body was taken on a ride that was also stimulating her mind. The pressure of her pearl being cornered and locked into place turned her on even more. Each time she moved a pulsating wave powered through her body.

Now standing to his feet he wrapped his right hand around and pressed up against her breasts for added stimulation, while taking his left hand and guiding his length and thickness close to her plump and throbbing wet place of passion. The top of his manhood teased and caressing up against her. Her heart was pounding just as her breath was picking up, panting and trapped in this position of intense pleasure.

"You want to back into it?" he said, holding her tightly and making the ropes constrict, adding even more pleasure. Her hips attempted to gyrate back to where she could feel the tip of his thickness that was sliding up and down on the outside of her V. Each time she went back, she could feel this rushing feeling of orgasms racing through her body, only to halt each time she tried to keep the ball locked between her legs.

"Aaaah, I want it; aaaaah, I want it, mmmmh, mmmmh," she moaned as her head went back and forth embracing these never before felt feelings.

He continued rubbing himself on her place of

passion, making her continuously attempt to back into it, wanting all of his thickness inside of her. She could feel the pressure of his manhood pressing up against her each time, allowing her to know how thick it was. At the same time her mind and body was taken over by this as she was clenching the cool steel of the dip bar her hands were secured to, imaging this was all of him in her grasp. The thoughts alone were turning her on even more, making her thrust her hips back. The tip of him entering made her let out a loud moan. "Aaaaaaaaaah, aaaaaaaaah, I want it! Aaaaaaah, aaaaaah," she let out, feeling her legs trembling from the pulsating stimulation that was making her feel like she was ready to have an orgasmic explosion as he took full control, pressing the tip of his manhood inside of her.

"Hold still, don't move, don't let the ball go."

"Mmmmmmh, oooooh give it to me, aaaaah, aaaaah," she moaned, feeling his hand come down off her breast and onto the exposed pearl locked between the ropes. He started caressing it with fast magic fingers, making orgasmic butterflies stir inside of her. His fingers going faster and faster made the sensitive pearl squirm, trying to evade his grasp to no avail.

"Aaaaaah, aaaaah, please, please, give it to me, please," she let out, breathing heavily and holding her position as he instructed her. At the same time, her heart and mind was racing just as the uncontrollable feeling of orgasms soared through her. She knew she couldn't hold it back even if she tried. Here it came. Right then her moan intensified as the ball released from her grip and she backed into him. As his thickness stretched her body, she let out a moan-like cry. "Aaaaah! Oooh my God, aaaaaaah, mmmmmh, mmmmmh." He pulled out of her wanting to still have control. Her body did feel good to him, but his mental game of the chase stimulated him more than the actual act of intercourse.

"Aaaaaah, what are you doing? Please give it to me, mmmmh, mmmmh," she moaned as her body was still releasing. He continued with his finger over her pearl until her moans shifted to intense breathing. Then he stopped, leaving her hanging on that sexual cliff of the ultimate climax.

He untied the ropes that had fallen to the floor. She let out a sigh of passion and looked down at her V and pearl that were soaked from her storm of orgasms. He came around in front of her still in the nude, allowing her to take all of him in visually. She would never forget this picturesque moment of him or what he had just done to her mind, heart, and body.

"You look like a woman who has taken control of finding her destiny," he said, smiling and untying her hands. She placed the first one on his shoulder, caressing him as he untied the other hand.

"You just tease the hell out of me, my body, and my mind," she said, looking with eyes of lust backed by a smile of satisfaction. Her other hand came free, and she caressed his chest. He took her hands into his as he closed in on her, coming close to her face.

"It's only a tease if you didn't reach the point of release, and from my count and feeling your flow over my fingertips and hearing your moans, you didn't sound left out or teased to me," he said, placing a kiss on her cheek before ending this erotic workout session. "I look forward to seeing you Monday," he said. With today being Friday she didn't want to wait that long to see him again. She wanted her next class to start right now or in the shower at her hotel room.

"Monday? I can't see you before that to finish what you started?" she asked, taking his hand so he could feel her affection.

"There's no intrigue in going all in too soon. I'm not going anywhere. I'll be here Monday. This gives me the entire weekend to think about how to keep you entertained physically, ment-ally, and emotionally. Since this is what you truly desire, right?" he said, walking around her and getting his things to get dressed. She did the same, bending over to get her clothes and letting out a moan, feeling so sensitive from his touch and holding the ball tightly between her legs. "Don't worry, you too will have enough thoughts of me and this very moment to get you through this weekend."

They gathered their things and exited the gym. He headed back to his condo to get cleaned up, eat, collect his thoughts, and reach out to his boys, Monty and SK, to exchange information on business and what they had discovered.

NINE

Jaelen, along with his buddies, met up at his condo. On his ride home he forgot about Tanya until she called him up reminding him about them meeting up after class. He put her off, promising her more excitement, for her patience. Right now, he needed to take care of something with his friends. She understood, knowing business was important. Little did she know this business he and his friends were taking care of involved her and other women.

They were all in the living room of the condo with their laptops and cell phones out going over the financials of the women they were plotting on: Paula Snyder, whose fiancé was a successful car dealer having $2.4 million net worth; Danna Liuen, whose husband was a self-made millionaire with his chain of grocery stores making him worth $9.3 million; and then Tanya, who had recently inherited $14.2 million after her father passed away. These were the women

Jaelen had set his eyes on, assisted by his friends Monty and SK. They took turns luring women in that crossed their paths, only to con them out of their riches, since they didn't seem to appreciate the men they were with enough to enjoy the lifestyles they had. Jaelen also had his eye on Laila, since she came across as hard to get. This made him want her even more, and at the same time he wanted to get into her husband's finances to see what he was worth these days. However, Monty and SK couldn't access this as they'd done with the other women already.

The way it worked with them, they would wipe each account clean, forwarding the money to offshore accounts that would later send it to the Bahamian Islands. One of them would fly down and retrieve the money, only to cash the check once they returned to America, making it look like an investor had given them the money. The key to making this work was doing it all at the same time without a trace or hint that they were the cause of this sudden bankruptcy. This was why Jaelen gravitated toward seducing these women who came to him yearning for the attention they were neglected of in their relationships. As for Tanya, she yearned for the attention of any man to see her as she truly desired. Jaelen just so happened to be on her radar since she joined his class, not realizing she had thrown herself into his web of erotic deception.

"I don't know why we can't access the Falcones' accounts and info," Monty said, since he was good at hacking into systems using the information most women give with their credit cards, addresses, phone numbers, jobs, and next of kin info. These things allowed them to backtrack and filter through it all, finding exactly what they were looking for.

"It's something about how they have everything set up. Plus, you know her husband is fully aware of cyber hacks and attacks. He also worked on Wall Street, so he knows the latest and can get the latest counter software, giving him the security and protection he needs," SK stated.

"For every action, there's a reaction. The same with technology. Every security measure has a countermeasure. We just have to figure out exactly what they have and how we can get in," Jaelen said, thinking about how he needed to get through to Laila. She seemed like she was going to be hard to break down and get through to, since she resisted him, not giving into him as the others had done so easily.

"It's time you step your game up, Jae," SK said. "She wants it; you just have to be the one to make her ask without her feeling compromised to lose everything she has. You said her husband is in Tokyo, right?"

"That's what her friends at the class said."

"We can use that info to track where the money came from for the ticket," Monty said, thinking as he tapped away on his laptop accessing the airport's info: ticket sales, where they came from, and who purchased them. He punched in Laila's husband's name. Nothing. "This isn't good."

"What?" Jaelen asked.

"There's no ticket purchased under his name."

"Punch in her name," SK said. Each of their minds started racing trying to figure out what was going on.

Monty punched in Laila's info to see if she had purchased a ticket with the airline. Nothing. Monty's eyebrows shifted as he raised up from looking at the screen. "This don't look good, fellas," he said, looking confused. He couldn't give up. Too much money was on the line. "No ticket in her name either."

"Maybe he didn't go to Tokyo as he may have wanted her to believe," Jaelen said, thinking steps ahead as he would do in a situation like that. "So if he did fly out from that airport, he may have used another name."

"Or he had someone else pick him up from the airport and take him to the destination of choice," SK said.

"He had to have a mistress," Monty added.

Jaelen leaned back on the couch processing

this situation that he needed to get in control of in order for it all to come together. Then it came to him.

"We need to find out who his mistress is. He has to trust her to an extent. If he does like I think he does, then she'll have financial information we could use. So before the night is over with, I want you to get into the cameras at the airport. If you need inside help, contact B-Moe from uptown. He still works as the security guard there. He can get you into all of the cameras. He owes us a favor," Jaelen instructed his team, feeling better about this situation he was feeling slipping from his grasp. "In the meantime, keep all eyes on the other women in case anything changes or doesn't look normal. That's all for now," he said, standing up at the same time his phone went off alerting him. It was the sound of his set reminder to tend to clients or take care of things in his daily schedule. He took a glance at his phone, accessing the reminder and realizing he had forgotten about the client Deborah gave him earlier today. He checked his watch seeing that it was 5:35 p.m. The appointment was for 5:30 p.m., and he was late, something he didn't normally do, being a punctual person.

The client was Laila Patrones-Falcone. Seeing this for the first time caught him off guard because he started thinking about her husband's alleged trip to Tokyo and her being alone and wanting him to come by. "What's going on here?" he wondered. Another thought entered his mind as he was walking his boys to the door.

"Laila is my five thirty house call. How crazy is this?" Jaelen said.

"This might be what we need to get what we want. Tens of millions is on the line, my friend, so stay focused," Monty said.

"Yeah, don't get too caught up in all of them

fly words and sayings you be spitting out, 'cause

you might confuse yourself, playboy," SK said,

laughing as he made his way out. Jaelen shut

the door, rushing to get his things, partially

excited about what was to come with her if

everything went as he desired.

Little did he know, he was about to get a lot

more than he had bargained for.

To Be Continued

To order books, please fill out the order form below:

To order films please go to www.good2gofilms.com

Name:_____

Address:_____

City:_____State:_____Zip Code: _____

Phone:_____

Email:_____

Method of Payment: Check   VISA MASTERCARD

Credit Card#:_ _____

Name as it appears on card: _____

Signature: _____

Item Name	Price	Qty	Amount
48 Hours to Die – Silk White	$14.99		
A Hustler's Dream – Ernest Morris	$14.99		
A Hustler's Dream 2 – Ernest Morris	$14.99		
A Thug's Devotion – J. L. Rose and J. M. McMillon	$14.99		
All Eyes on Tommy Gunz – Warren Holloway	$14.99		
Black Reign – Ernest Morris	$14.99		
Bloody Mayhem Down South – Trayvon Jackson	$14.99		
Bloody Mayhem Down South 2 – Trayvon Jackson	$14.99		
Business Is Business – Silk White	$14.99		
Business Is Business 2 – Silk White	$14.99		
Business Is Business 3 – Silk White	$14.99		
Cash In Cash Out – Assa Raymond Baker	$14.99		
Cash In Cash Out 2 – Assa Raymond Baker	$14.99		
Childhood Sweethearts – Jacob Spears	$14.99		
Childhood Sweethearts 2 – Jacob Spears	$14.99		
Childhood Sweethearts 3 – Jacob Spears	$14.99		
Childhood Sweethearts 4 – Jacob Spears	$14.99		
Connected To The Plug – Dwan Marquis Williams	$14.99		
Connected To The Plug 2 – Dwan Marquis Williams	$14.99		
Connected To The Plug 3 – Dwan Williams	$14.99		
Cost of Betrayal – W.C. Holloway	$14.99		
Cost of Betrayal 2 – W.C. Holloway	$14.99		
Deadly Reunion – Ernest Morris	$14.99		
Dream's Life – Assa Raymond Baker	$14.99		
Flipping Numbers – Ernest Morris	$14.99		

Item Name	Price	Qty	Amount
Flipping Numbers 2 – Ernest Morris	$14.99		
He Loves Me, He Loves You Not – Mychea	$14.99		
He Loves Me, He Loves You Not 2 – Mychea	$14.99		
He Loves Me, He Loves You Not 3 – Mychea	$14.99		
He Loves Me, He Loves You Not 4 – Mychea	$14.99		
He Loves Me, He Loves You Not 5 – Mychea	$14.99		
Killing Signs – Ernest Morris	$14.99		
Killing Signs 2 – Ernest Morris	$14.99		
Kings of the Block – Dwan Willams	$14.99		
Kings of the Block 2 – Dwan Willams	$14.99		
Lord of My Land – Jay Morrison	$14.99		
Lost and Turned Out – Ernest Morris	$14.99		
Love & Dedication – W.C. Holloway	$14.99		
Love Hates Violence – De'Wayne Maris	$14.99		
Love Hates Violence 2 – De'Wayne Maris	$14.99		
Love Hates Violence 3 – De'Wayne Maris	$14.99		
Love Hates Violence 4 – De'Wayne Maris	$14.99		
Married To Da Streets – Silk White	$14.99		
M.E.R.C. – Make Every Rep Count Health and Fitness	$14.99		
Mercenary In Love – J.L. Rose & J.L. Turner	$14.99		
Money Make Me Cum – Ernest Morris	$14.99		
My Besties – Asia Hill	$14.99		
My Besties 2 – Asia Hill	$14.99		
My Besties 3 – Asia Hill	$14.99		
My Besties 4 – Asia Hill	$14.99		
My Boyfriend's Wife – Mychea	$14.99		
My Boyfriend's Wife 2 – Mychea	$14.99		
My Brothers Envy – J. L. Rose	$14.99		
My Brothers Envy 2 – J. L. Rose	$14.99		
Naughty Housewives – Ernest Morris	$14.99		
Naughty Housewives 2 – Ernest Morris	$14.99		
Naughty Housewives 3 – Ernest Morris	$14.99		
Naughty Housewives 4 – Ernest Morris	$14.99		
Never Be The Same – Silk White	$14.99		

Item Name	Price	Qty	Amount
Scarred Faces – Assa Raymond Baker	$14.99		
Scarred Knuckles – Assa Raymond Baker	$14.99		
Shades of Revenge – Assa Raymond Baker	$14.99		
Slumped – Jason Brent	$14.99		
Someone's Gonna Get It – Mychea	$14.99		
Stranded – Silk White	$14.99		
Supreme & Justice – Ernest Morris	$14.99		
Supreme & Justice 2 – Ernest Morris	$14.99		
Supreme & Justice 3 – Ernest Morris	$14.99		
Tears of a Hustler – Silk White	$14.99		
Tears of a Hustler 2 – Silk White	$14.99		
Tears of a Hustler 3 – Silk White	$14.99		
Tears of a Hustler 4– Silk White	$14.99		
Tears of a Hustler 5 – Silk White	$14.99		
Tears of a Hustler 6 – Silk White	$14.99		
The Excitement I Bring – Warren Holloway	$14.99		
The Excitement I Bring 2 – Warren Holloway	$14.99		
The Last Love Letter – Warren Holloway	$14.99		
The Last Love Letter 2 – Warren Holloway	$14.99		
The Panty Ripper – Reality Way	$14.99		
The Panty Ripper 3 – Reality Way	$14.99		
The Solution – Jay Morrison	$14.99		
The Teflon Queen – Silk White	$14.99		
The Teflon Queen 2 – Silk White	$14.99		
The Teflon Queen 3 – Silk White	$14.99		
The Teflon Queen 4 – Silk White	$14.99		
The Teflon Queen 5 – Silk White	$14.99		
The Teflon Queen 6 – Silk White	$14.99		
The Vacation – Silk White	$14.99		
Tied To A Boss – J.L. Rose	$14.99		
Tied To A Boss 2 – J.L. Rose	$14.99		
Tied To A Boss 3 – J.L. Rose	$14.99		
Tied To A Boss 4 – J.L. Rose	$14.99		
Tied To A Boss 5 – J.L. Rose	$14.99		
Time Is Money – Silk White	$14.99		

Item Name	Price	Qty	Amount
Tomorrow's Not Promised – Robert Torres	$14.99		
Tomorrow's Not Promised 2 – Robert Torres	$14.99		
Two Mask One Heart – Jacob Spears and Trayvon Jackson	$14.99		
Two Mask One Heart 2 – Jacob Spears and Trayvon Jackson	$14.99		
Two Mask One Heart 3 – Jacob Spears and Trayvon Jackson	$14.99		
Wrong Place Wrong Time – Silk White	$14.99		
Young Goonz – Reality Way	$14.99		
Subtotal:			
Tax:			
Shipping (Free) U.S. Media Mail:			
Total:			

Make Checks Payable To: Good2Go Publishing, 7311 W Glass Lane, Laveen, AZ 85339